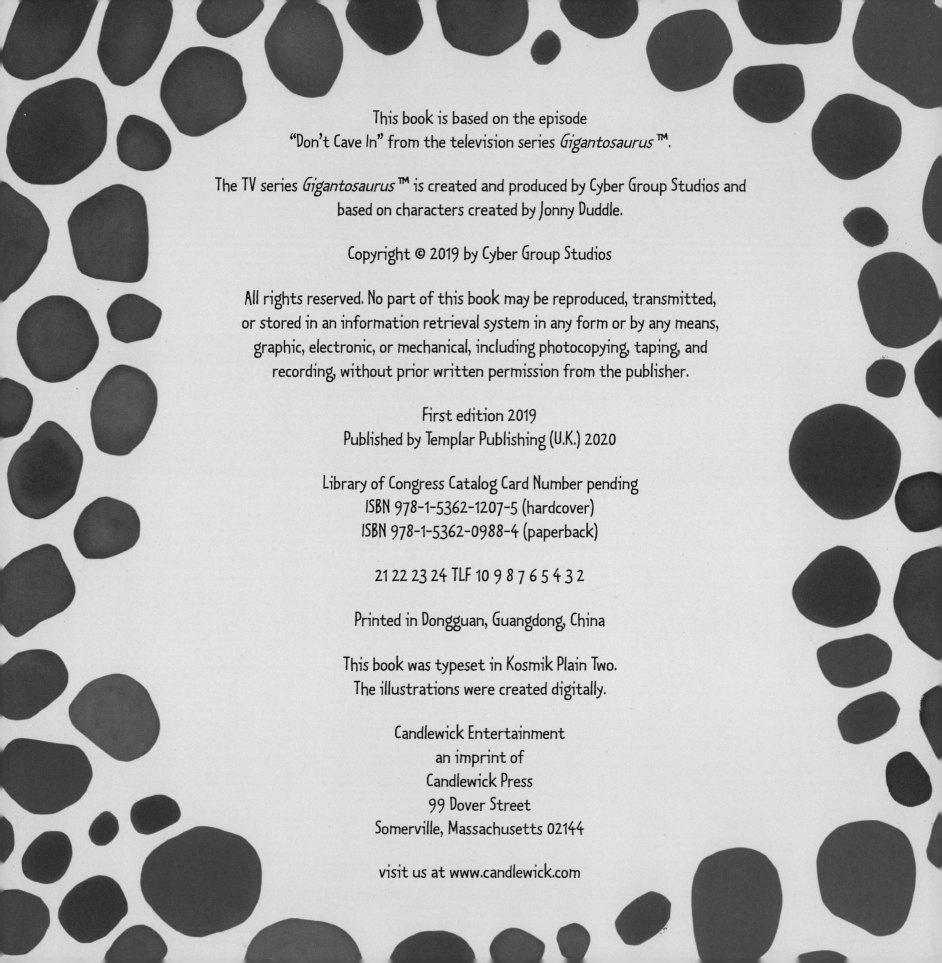

First edition 2019
Published by Templar Publishing (U.K.) 2020

Library of Congress Catalog Card Number pending
ISBN 978-1-5362-1207-5 (hardcover)
ISBN 978-1-5362-0988-4 (paperback)

21 22 23 24 TLF 10 9 8 7 6 5 4 3 2

Printed in Dongguan, Guangdong, China

This book was typeset in Kosmik Plain Two.
The illustrations were created digitally.

Candlewick Entertainment
an imprint of
Candlewick Press
99 Dover Street
Somerville, Massachusetts 02144

visit us at www.candlewick.com

GIGANTOSAURUS™

DON'T CAVE IN

CANDLEWICK
ENTERTAINMENT

In a clearing deep in the jungle, dinosaurs Tiny and Bill stood trembling with fear. Trey, Tiny's big brother, was telling them the scariest story they had ever heard.

"So this is where it happened," Trey began, "deep in the CAVE OF SHRIEKS."

The little dinos gasped and peered into the dark cave.

Trey continued. "This is where I came face-to-face with . . . SHRIEKASAURUS!"

Shriekasaurus is soooo scary.

Ignatius had been listening to Trey's story.
He crept out from the trees.

"You really DO NOT want to go into that cave!" he warned.
Tiny and Bill agreed. It didn't seem like a place for little dinos.

The friends stood nervously outside the cave's entrance.

Trey and Ignatius had only just walked away when Rocky and
Mazu came charging up the jungle path.

The ground rumbled and trees shook. That could mean only one thing. . . .

GIGANTOSAURUS!

"Quick!" shouted Mazu, dragging Tiny, Rocky, and Bill into the cave. "Hide in here!"

Gigantosaurus stomped right up to the cave entrance, but he was too big to fit inside. He let out a deafening roar.

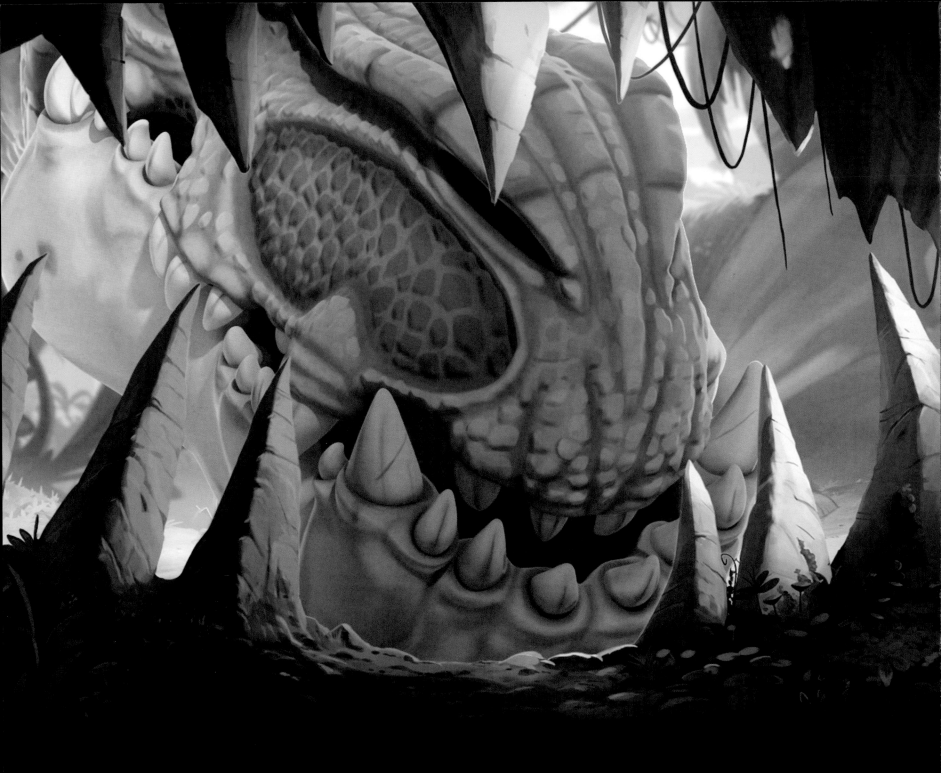

The enormous dinosaur sniffed curiously around the cave entrance. At least the little dinos were safe . . . for now.

"We'd better look for another way out," said Mazu, leading her friends deeper inside.

The cave was gloomy and dark — how would they ever find their way back? Luckily, Mazu knew just what to do. She reached for a long purple plant.

"This cave has its very own glow sticks!" she said excitedly.

Mazu shook the strange plant. *PING!* It lit up.

Mazu led the way through the cave.

"I sure hope that we don't run into Shriekasaurus," said Tiny, remembering what Trey had told them.

"He's mean," cried Bill, looking left and right. "So mean!"

"That's weird," said Mazu thoughtfully. "How come I've never heard of this Shriekasaurus?"

At that moment, a screeching roar echoed through the cave.

The little dinos squealed. Now everyone was scared!

RAARRRGHH!

Tiny looked around at her terrified friends — she had to do something to help! She took a deep breath, then started to sing a song. It wasn't long before Bill, Mazu, and Rocky joined in, too.

"Thanks, Tiny," said Mazu gratefully. "I feel better now."

Suddenly, another piercing roar rumbled through the gloom. The friends looked up and saw Shriekasaurus's huge, spiky TEETH!

"Wait a minute," said Tiny, heading straight toward the frightening fangs. "It's just a shadow." She poked a glow stick and the toothy shadow wobbled.

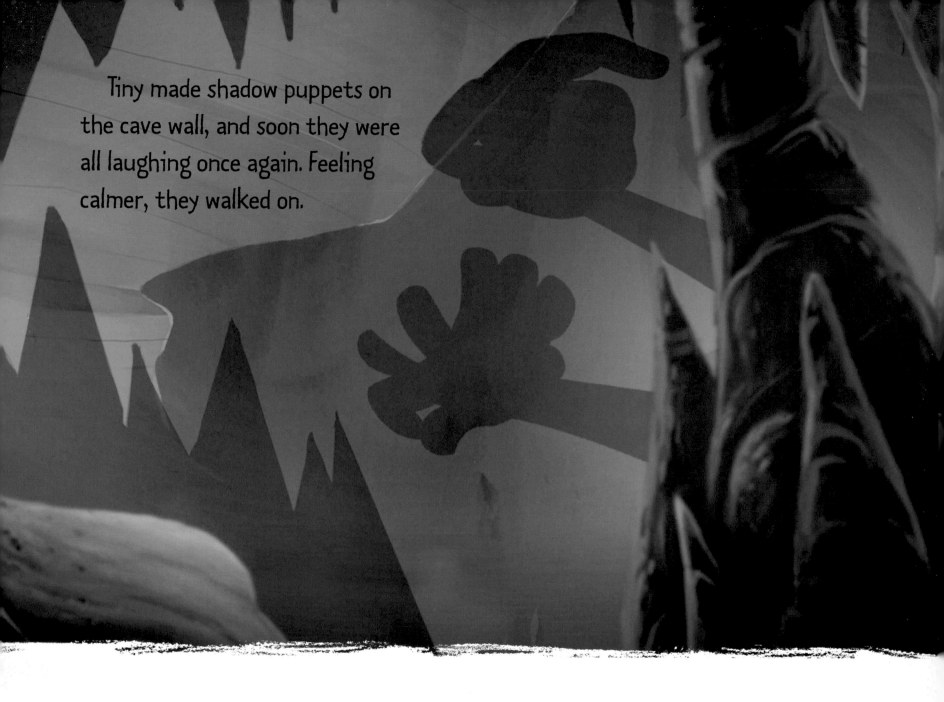

Tiny made shadow puppets on the cave wall, and soon they were all laughing once again. Feeling calmer, they walked on.

"WHOA!" the friends yelled as they suddenly went tumbling down a steep slope.

They landed in the middle of an underground lake. They were trapped! It seemed the only way out was across the lake's wobbly stepping stones.

"Tiny, you go first," Rocky insisted.

Bill agreed. "You're our fearless leader!"

But Tiny shook her head. "I'm not fearless!
I'm as scared as you are. I've just been trying
to forget about that and think of silly stuff."

Her friends couldn't believe what they were
hearing. Tiny had been so brave!

But what about
the puppet show?
And the song?

I'm still scared
on the inside.

"We couldn't have made it this far without you, Tiny," said Mazu proudly.

Tiny smiled. Her friends really believed in her. Suddenly, she felt much braver. "Let's get through this together!" she said.

Don't cave in now!

Tiny leapt onto the first wobbly stepping stone. She jumped across the lake from stone to stone, but just as she got to the other side, she slipped and fell out of sight.

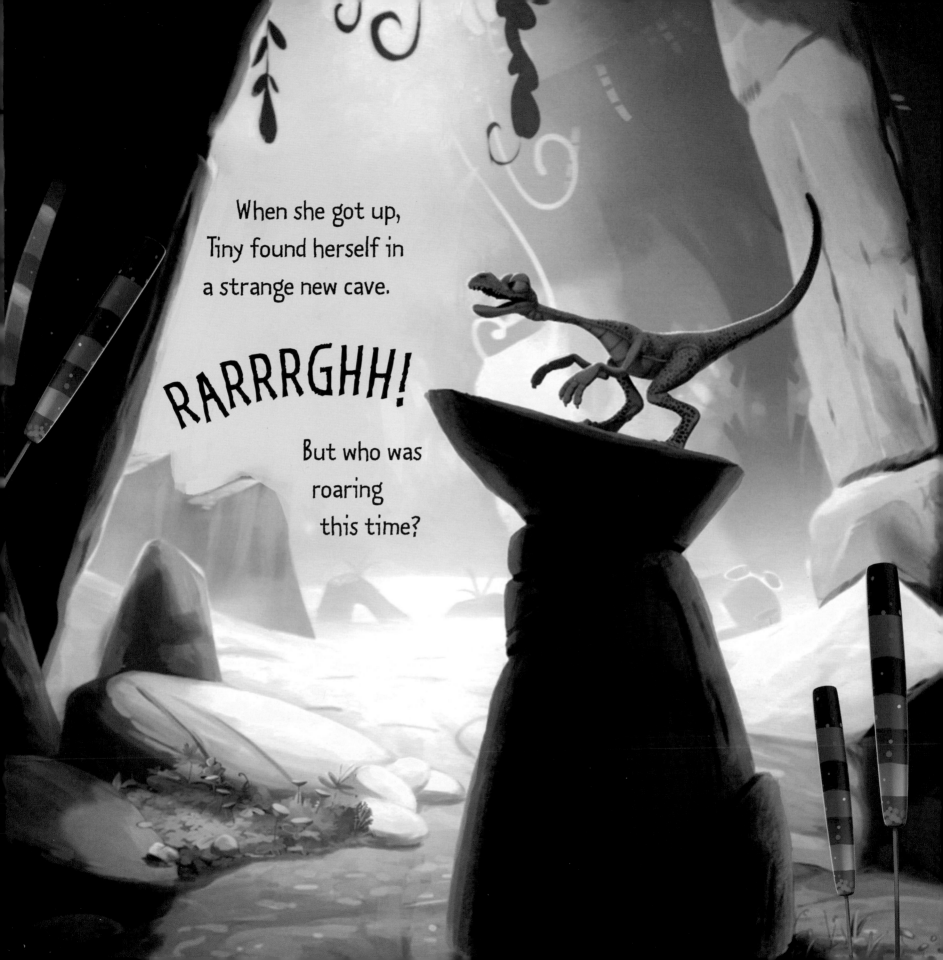

When she got up,
Tiny found herself in
a strange new cave.

RARRRGHH!

But who was
roaring
this time?

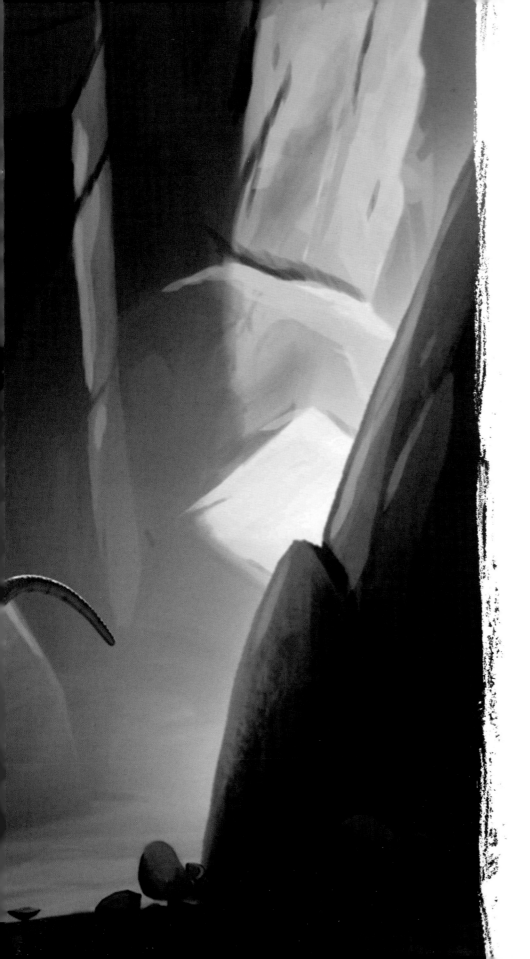

It was Ignatius! As soon as he spotted Tiny, the little yellow dinosaur stopped roaring.

He laughed nervously. "I guess I can't lie anymore. . . . I'm Shriekasaurus."

"But why?" asked Tiny.

"I'm just protecting my hangout from baby dinos," he replied. "But I can't believe you made it this far!"

Ignatius was impressed with Tiny's bravery. "Check this out," he said as he led her through a crack between the rocks.

Ignatius's secret hangout was the most beautiful sight Tiny had ever seen.

Mazu, Bill, and Rocky scrambled into the new cave, too, ready to save their friend from the fearsome Shriekasaurus. But they had nothing to worry about.

"Look," said Tiny, pointing to the curly slides and bubbling hot springs. "It was totally worth not caving in."

"Awesome!" cheered the little dinos. They couldn't wait to explore.

They whizzed down slides, climbed on rocks, and floated in pools. Bill sniffed the air curiously — what was that glorious smell?

Ignatius chuckled and pointed to a bunch of golden cave moss hanging above them. "It's pretty tasty, too," he said.

Just then, Tiny had a brilliant idea. "I bet that's what Gigantosaurus was looking for," she began. "Let's bring him some cave moss!"

When the friends finally left the cave, the big dinos wanted to hear all about their adventure.

Trey listened, looking very sheepish. "I never actually went in," he finally admitted. Tiny looked up at him in shock, wondering why Trey would have lied.

I just wanted to sound tough!

All of a sudden, the dinosaurs heard a familiar TERRIFYING roar
rip through the trees, and Tiny knew she had just one last job to do . . .

leave some tasty cave moss out for Gigantosaurus!